This Little Tiger book belongs to:

_____

_____

_____

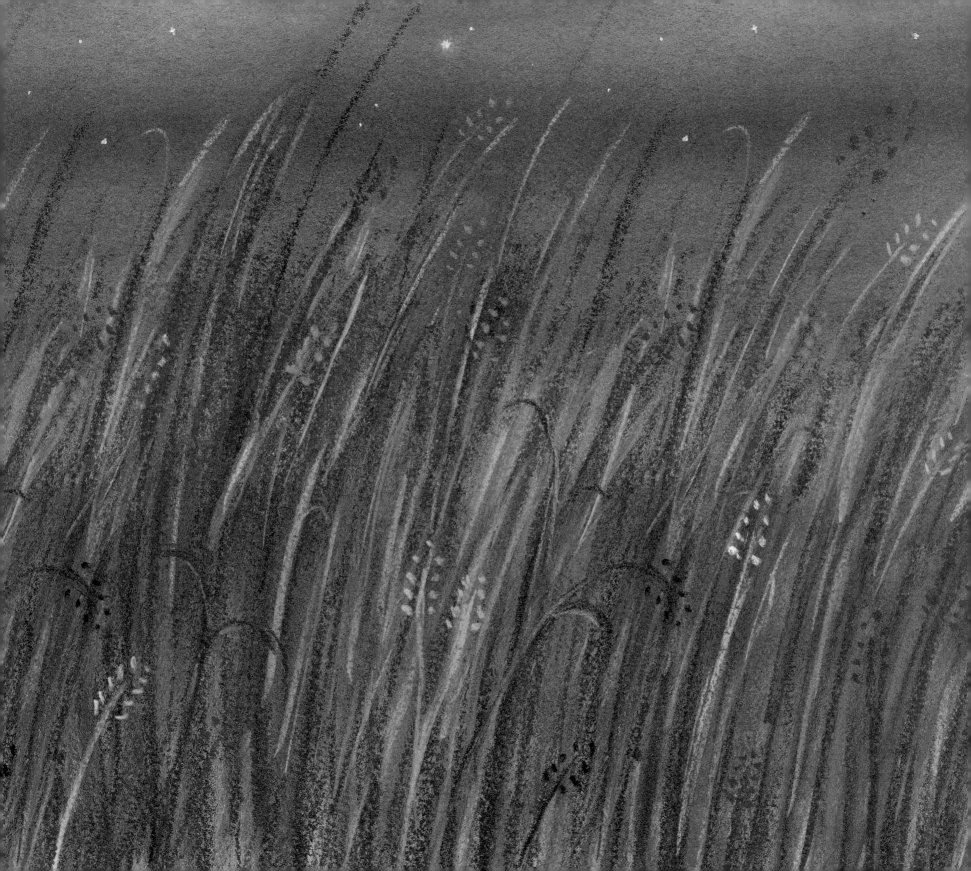

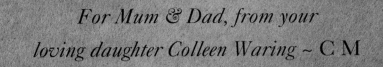

For Mum & Dad, from your
loving daughter Colleen Waring ~ C M

LITTLE TIGER PRESS LTD,
an imprint of the Little Tiger Group
1 The Coda Centre, 189 Munster Road, London SW6 6AW
www.littletiger.co.uk

First published in Great Britain 2008
This edition published 2009

A CIP catalogue record for this book is available from the British Library

Printed in China • LTP/1400/1878/0417

ISBN 978-1-84506-758-8

2 4 6 8 10 9 7 5 3 1

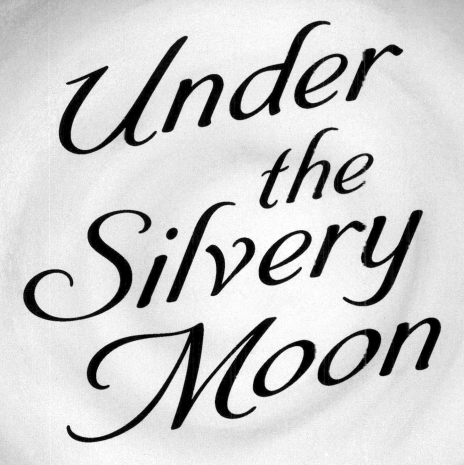

Under the Silvery Moon

Colleen McKeown

LiTTLE TiGER

LONDON

The stars were shining brightly.
Little kitten was in bed.
But up he sat, still wide awake,
"Sleep now," his mother said.

"But it's so noisy, I can't sleep!"
said kitten, with a cry.
"It's just our friends," said mother cat.
"They're waking up nearby . . .

The tiny mice are playing;
    they explore the barn at night.
They skip and scamper here and there,
    beneath the warm lamplight.

Hush, kitten, can you hear it,
that shuffling, snuffling sound?
The hedgehogs look for food to eat
along the moonlit ground.

That cry you hear, so long and loud,
that distant, haunting tune,
Belongs to fox who's up at night.
He's calling to the moon.

Around us swirls a summer song;
 it's whispered through the trees.
The evening wind is blowing
 through the softly rustling leaves.

Beyond the midnight meadow,
 where the air is soft and cool,
The frogs are gently croaking
 all around the moonlit pool.

Some creatures are not stirring;
    they do not make a peep.
Like us they've had a busy day,
    and now they're fast asleep.

The badgers stretch their sturdy legs,
and blink into the dark.
'Good evening,' they are calling,
with a deep and playful bark.

The nimble hares are dancing;
their paws thump on the ground.
With joyful leaps they chase their tails
and spring and dart around.

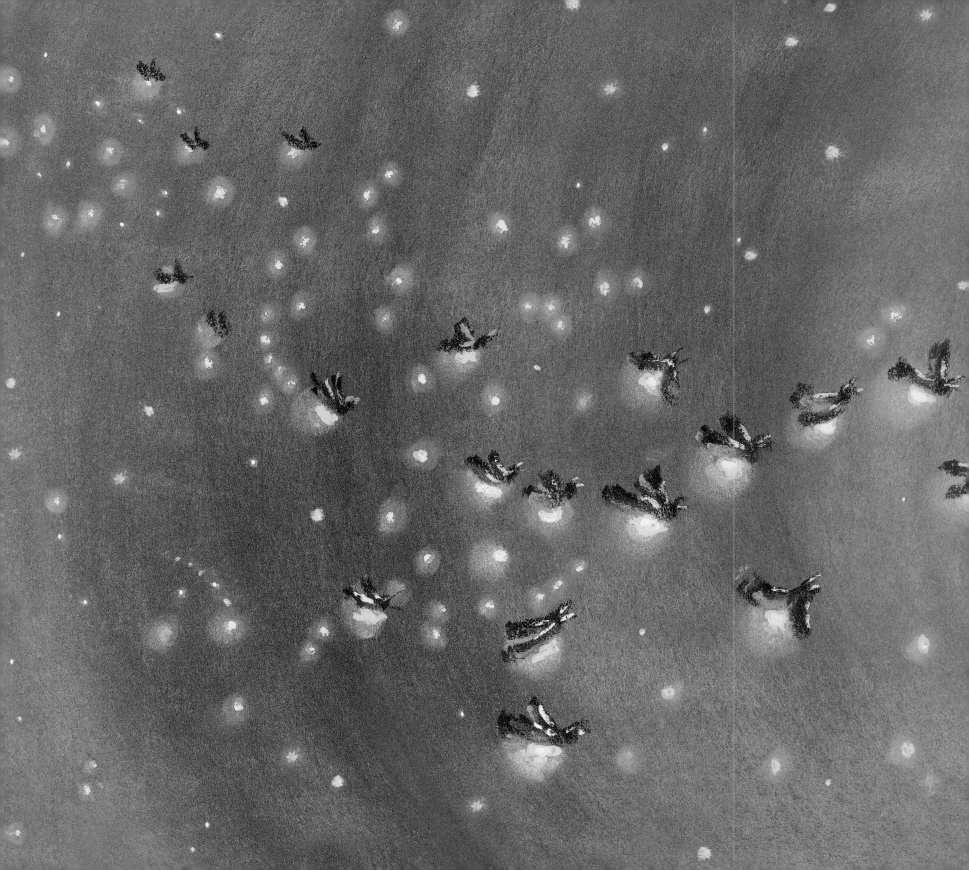

Something quiet and gentle
   lights up the dark, night skies.
Glowing warm and lovely
   are the dreamy fireflies.

Owl is hooting softly;
    across the stars she glides.
Soaring home towards the barn,
    upon the wind she rides.

And so you see, my little one,
    there's nothing you should fear.
Our friends' night-time adventures
    are all that you can hear."

Little kitten closed his eyes
    and hugged his mother tight.
"It's time you went to sleep," she purred.
    "Sweet dreams, my love, goodnight."

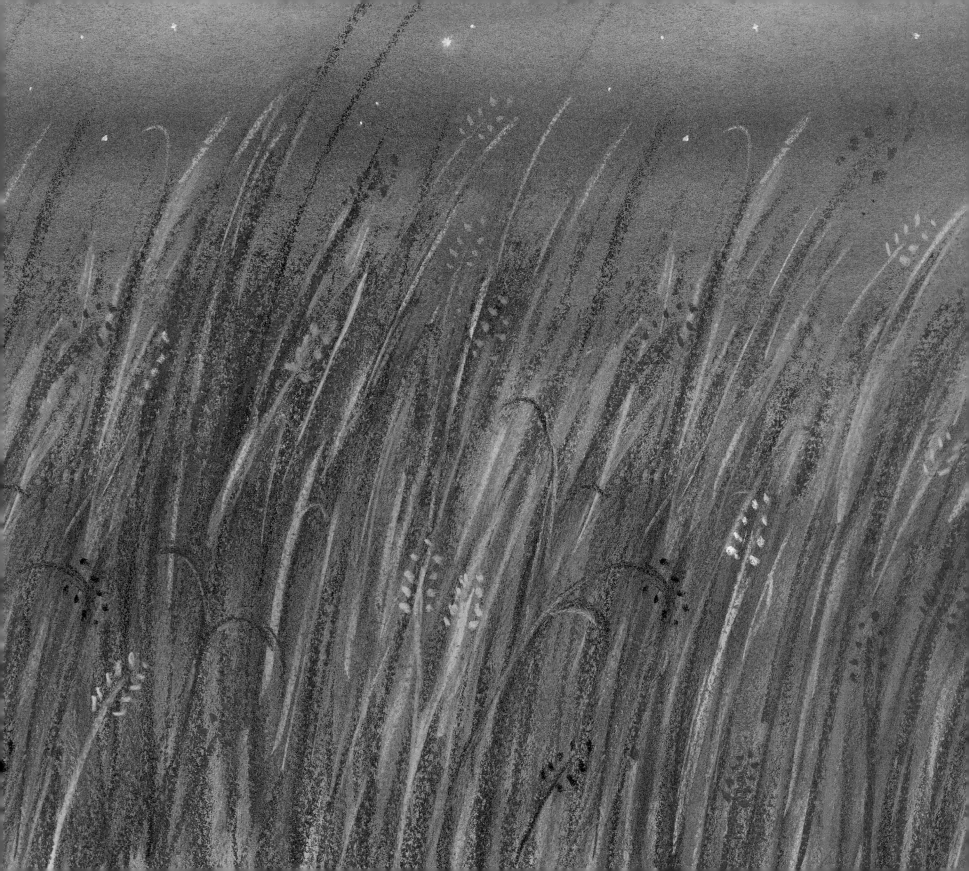

More fabulous books from Little Tiger Press!

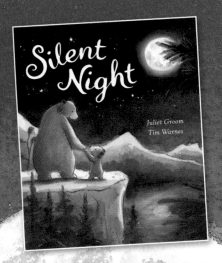

Silent Night

Juliet Groom
Tim Warnes

The Wishing Star

M Christina Butler   Frank Endersby

Time to Sleep, Alfie Bear!

Catherine Walters

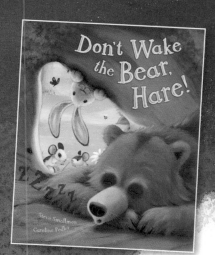

Don't Wake the Bear, Hare!

Steve Smallman
Caroline Pedler

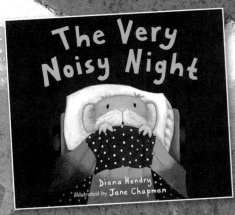

The Very Noisy Night

Diana Hendry
illustrated by Jane Chapman

Under the Silvery Moon

COLLEEN McKEOWN

For information regarding any of the above titles
or for our catalogue, please contact us:

Little Tiger Press, 1 The Coda Centre, 189 Munster Road, London SW6 6AW

Tel: 020 7385 6333 • Email: contact@littletiger.co.uk • www.littletiger.co.uk

Image taken from *Silent Night* copyright © Tim Warnes 2010

Visit Tim Warnes at www.ChapmanandWarnes.com